REGULAR GUY

REGULAR GUY
SARAH WEEKS

A LAURA GERINGER BOOK

An Imprint of HarperCollins*Publishers*

Library of Congress Cataloging-in-Publication Data
Weeks, Sarah.
    Regular Guy / Sarah Weeks.
        p.   cm.
    "A Laura Geringer book."
    Summary: Because he is so different from his eccentric parents, twelve-year-old Guy is
convinced he has been switched at birth with a classmate whose parents seem more normal.
    ISBN 0-06-028367-X. — ISBN 0-06-028368-8 (lib. bdg.)
    [1. Parent and child—Fiction.   2. Identity—Fiction.]   I. Title.
PZ7.W42215Rg   1999   99-12118
[Fic]—dc21   CIP
                                                                                    AC

Typography by Al Cetta   1   2   3   4   5   6   7   8   9   10   ❖   First edition

For Gabriel

(and Ms. Janover's 1997–98 6th grade Humanities class)

CHAPTER ONE

"I know it's a long shot, but I don't feel I can just eliminate the possibility that I was raised by wolves without at least considering it for a second, do you?"

"You're touched in the head, you know that, Strang? Positively touched."

I count on my best friend, Buzz, to be honest with me. We've known each other since second grade, when he moved to Cedar Springs from some place down South. Most of his accent is gone by now, but his twang still shows through a little, especially when he gets what he calls "riled up."

"Do you really think it's out of the question?" I asked seriously.

"Well, do you howl at the moon, Guy?"

"No."

"Have cravings for raw jackrabbit?"

"Definitely not."

"Lick yourself?"

"Never," I said.

"Okay, then I think it's safe to say we can rule out the wolf theory."

"Wait a minute, Buzzard. Did you ever consider the possibility that maybe it was so weird and horrible out there in the wild with my wolf-pack family that I just can't let myself remember it?"

"In that case, maybe you'd better consider the possibility that you were actually raised by possums, Guy, not wolves. I mean, just because you don't hang by your tail and play dead now doesn't mean you didn't used to, right?"

"Aw, shut up."

"Anything you say, possum boy."

We sat there in silence for a minute.

Finally I announced, "Last night at dinner

my father did the oyster trick again."

"Oh, man. Were you home at least?"

"Nope. Right in the middle of the restaurant. 'Watch this,' he goes, 'watch what your old man can do, Guy.' Like I don't already know. Then before I can even look away he sticks it up his nose, sucks it up there with that horrible noise, and spits it out of his mouth."

"Gross me out the door!"

"I thought I was going to puke," I said. "My mother, of course, applauded."

"Did he stand up and make the announcement about how no one should attempt it at home?"

I nodded.

"Well, you know what I always say—just add an 'e' to Strang and look whatcha get. Man, you really can't go out in public with them, can you?" Buzz said.

"It's not like it's so much better being around them at home, either. Take a look in my sock drawer," I said.

"Which one is it?"

"Second from the top," I said as I watched Buzz pull open the drawer.

"What's the deal?" he asked as he pulled out a balled-up pair of unmatched socks.

"She's a firm believer in the idea that opposites attract."

"But, socks?" Buzz held up another mismatched pair.

"There's not one matched set in there. Open the top drawer."

"I'm afraid."

I laughed. Buzz opened the drawer and pulled out a pair of rainbow-colored underwear.

"Groovy, man. Very sixties!"

"She tie-dyed every pair of underwear in the house last week," I said with a sigh.

Just then there was a knock at the door. I groaned, flopped back on my bed, and waited for the inevitable. In she came, singing at the top of her lungs.

"Snicker Doodles, Snicker Doodles, rah

rah rah! Eat a bunch, hear 'em crunch, siss-boom-bah!"

My mother danced around the room, holding a plate up in the air like a fancy waiter. She had on lime-green stretch pants and a frilly Day-Glo orange top. Her curly mop of bright-red hair was pulled up into a ponytail, which she kept in place with a twist tie—the kind you use to close up garbage bags. She finished her song with a last wiggle of her rear end, set down the plate of lumpy cookies, and clicked out of the room in her favorite high heel shoes—the ones with the plastic tropical fish suspended in the see-through heels.

"Nice outfit, Mrs. Strang!" Buzz called as he reached for a cookie. He took a large bite and sang through his mouthful, "Snicker Doodles, Snicker Doodles, rah rah rah!"

"Can you picture your mother walking around in a getup like that, Buzz?" I asked as I slid a cookie off the plate. "I mean, put yourself in my place, can you imagine what it's like?"

Buzz just shook his head and crammed another cookie in his mouth.

"Maybe it was one of those mix-ups in the hospital where they give the wrong baby to the wrong mother," I said.

"Think that could really happen?" Buzz asked.

"Sure. I bet it happens all the time," I said.

"And you never know until you have a bad car accident and they call your parents to the hospital so they can give you a kidney or something and you find out you don't match up genetically, right?" asked Buzz.

"Yeah," I said, "I mean, do I even *look* like either of them?"

"Well, I've never actually seen you in stretch pants. . . ."

"Come on, Buzz, I'm serious. Do I bear any resemblance to them whatsoever?"

"None whatsoever."

"I swear, I don't think they're my real parents," I said.

"Well, they seem pretty convinced of it,"

Buzz said. "And you already asked about whether you were adopted, right?"

"Yeah, they denied it. But something's not right, Buzz. I can feel it in my bones."

"You mean, your kidneys."

"Goof on me if you want, Buzzard, but I know there's something fishy about this family."

"Whatever you say, Guy. Hey, do you want that last Snicker Doodle or can I scarf it?" Buzz asked as he reached for the cookie.

I didn't answer him. I couldn't think about cookies at a time like this. Somehow or other I had to come up with a way to uncover the truth about my origins. It wasn't going to be easy, but I couldn't stand it much longer. I needed to know who I really was.

CHAPTER TWO

"**W**hat's with the golfers?" Buzz asked.

"My mother thinks it's a manly sport, and since I'm her 'little man' . . ." I trailed off as if that was enough of an explanation.

"When did she do it?"

"Last night, after I went to sleep."

We were discussing my lunch box. The day before it had been an ordinary red plastic box with my name written on it in black Magic Marker, but my mother had been visited by one of her frequent creative urges and had decoupaged a bunch of pictures of golfers and golf equipment all over it. My mother *loves* to decoupage. The way you do it is you take some object and glue down pictures on it, then you paint over it with this liquid stuff that makes everything all shiny and smooth. You can do it to almost any-thing, trust me—I know. Another thing I know is that once it's dry, that's it—it doesn't come off no matter how much you want it to or how hard you work at it with a screwdriver.

"Who's that guy up by the handle?" Buzz asked.

"Lee Trevino," I said, reading the caption under the golfer caught in mid swing.

"Who's he?"

"Manly golfer, I guess," I said.

We snapped open our lunch boxes and flipped back the lids. I looked longingly at Buzz's peanut butter and jelly sandwich.

"Want to trade?" I asked.

"Whatcha got?" he said, peering into my lunch box.

"One raw hot dog, three grape kebobs, couple of garlic twists, and an apricot nectar."

"Sheesh." Buzz turned away and took a

bite of his sandwich.

He ended up taking pity on me and giving me half of his sandwich, which I washed down with the apricot nectar. Then we dismantled the grape kebobs, eating the grapes and piling the chunks of candied fruit she'd alternated with them on the toothpicks into a miniature pyramid. We used the garlic twists for footballs, shooting finger field goals at each other across the table. As always, I tossed the hot dog. Just because my mother thinks that a cold, raw wiener is the same thing as bologna doesn't mean I do.

"Any progress in the search for your roots?" Buzz asked as we headed out to the playground, where we normally spend the second half of our lunch period.

"Not yet. But I'm working on it."

"I've been thinking about that switched at birth thing some more," said Buzz. "The way I see it is that if that happened, whoever you got switched with would have to be exactly the same age as you, right?"

"Yeah, so?"

"Well, if they moved away, you're pretty much sunk, because it's very hard to track down people who traipse all over the world, especially if you don't even know their names. If they didn't move, though, couldn't that kid who's living with your real parents be right here under your nose?"

"You mean at school?"

"Yeah, he'd be in the sixth grade, just like you, right?"

"You know, you could be on to something there, Buzz."

"Your birthday's July fourteenth, right?"

"Uh huh."

"Well, I happen to know that there's a file in the office that has all that sort of stuff. You know—birthdays, addresses, allergies, and junk for every sixth grader in the school. All we have to do is take a look in there and see if anybody else has a birthday right around yours."

"How are we going to get into the file?"

"We gotta get detention."

"Detention?" My voice cracked on the word. I've never been sent down to the office for anything in my life. I'm a major do-gooder, and I can't remember a teacher ever even looking at me sideways, let alone sending me down for detention.

"Yep. We've got to do something bad enough to get us both sent down to the office. That way one of us can search the file while the other one distracts old Mrs. Dipnower."

The bell rang, and I went inside to French class. Buzz was taking Spanish, so I knew there was no point in trying to misbehave when I couldn't be assured that he'd get sent downstairs too. Next was a double period of Humanities. Buzz was already in his seat when I got there. He gave me a look like, "Get ready," as I took my place across the table from him.

My teacher, Mr. Glass, really likes me. He's always reading my papers out loud to show

how well I follow directions, and on the big homework chart I'm the only one who has check-pluses after every assignment. Maybe I'm not the most creative student in the world, but my work habits are pretty impressive, I guess. It wasn't going to be easy to rub him the wrong way. Buzz doesn't work quite as hard as me, but Mr. Glass likes him too, on account of his sense of humor. Buzz can write terrific stories. Like the one about the boy who eats a thesaurus for breakfast and starts using a million synonyms whenever he talks. That was a good one. Especially when he has to go to the bathroom and he says, "It is imperative that I espy a comfort station or I shall indubitably detonate."

We were studying Greek myths this term, so Mr. Glass started reading to us from *The Odyssey*. I was watching Melanie Mason doodle in the margins of her notebook. She was drawing horses with long flowing manes. A total girl thing, but still they were pretty realistic looking. Meanwhile, Mr. Glass was up to the part about the one-eyed monster and the soldiers hiding underneath the sheep. I felt Buzz kick me hard under the table. Looking up, I saw him tapping his pencil rapidly on the top of his paper. Written upside down so I could read it was: I HAVE A PLAN.

"What is it?" I mouthed to him.

FOLLOW MY LEAD, he wrote and then tapped the message again, more insistently this time.

"Who's making that tapping sound?" bellowed Mr. Glass as he glared around the room from table to table.

For a second I thought maybe this was the extent of Buzz's big plan, detention for table tapping, but when he didn't 'fess up, Mr. Glass resumed his reading aloud, and I waited nervously for my next instructions.

Turns out that Buzz's brilliant plan was that I was supposed to pretend to punch him in the nose. He had pinched a package of ketchup from the lunchroom and filled his hand with it. After I hit him he would smear the ketchup under his nose and off we'd go to detention for roughhousing. Well, what happened was that I couldn't seem to find the right moment to fake my punch. Buzz got antsy and tried to grab my hand and make me hit him, but his sleeve got caught on his binder ring and the ketchup squirted out all over Melanie's notebook, which sent her completely around the twist. She was steamed, but it worked out all right because I let her copy my notes while Buzz and I got sent down to the office for the second half of the period.

Once we were down there on the detention bench, Buzz whispered, "What do you want to do, snoop or distract?"

"Snoop, I guess," I said.

So Buzz sidled over to Mrs. Dipnower's desk, and I waited until he had her attention before sliding down the bench toward the tall green file cabinets.

"You know, Mrs. Dipnower, that brown

dress you're wearing puts me in mind of the exact color of the cattails my mama and I used to pull down in Louisiana when I was little."

I had to hold back my laughter. Buzz was laying on his southern accent something fierce. The words were dripping out of his mouth like honey and twanging around the room like old guitar strings, and much to my amazement, it seemed to be working.

"Why, Buzz, I don't believe I ever noticed your accent before. It's quite charming, really."

"Thank you kindly, Ma'am. So anyway, as I was saying, that color is a kissin' cousin to the shade of those cattails we used to pick when Mama took a mind to making her famous tickly-stick stew. Mmm-mmm nothin' like a bowl of tickly-stick stew with a biscuit to dunk in it and a couple of deep-fat-fried crawdads chunked on top for crunch."

I happen to know that Buzz's mom cooks regular stuff like macaroni and cheese and meatloaf, but Buzz's story was buying me plenty of time to slip off the bench and snag the sixth-grade records file out of the bottom drawer. I slipped it into my binder and eased back onto the bench.

While Buzz launched into some ridiculous tall tale about his grandpappy (who, by the way, is a retired stockbroker) getting a 'gator baby tangled up in his long johns, I flipped through the pages until I found what I wanted. Or anyway, what I was looking for. When I'd managed to stick the file back in the drawer I signaled Buzz that our mission was accomplished, and he cut his story short by slapping his knee and laughing like a fool. Mrs. Dipnower was eating it up with a spoon, and I think she may have been disappointed when Buzz came back and joined me on the bench.

"Did you get it?" he whispered.

I nodded.

"What's the matter, Guy? You look like you saw a ghost."

I handed him the sheet of paper on which
I'd written the name of the one sixth grader
who shared my birthday.

"Holy crow," he said with appropriate
feeling.

Just then the bell for final period rang
and Mrs. Dipnower released us from our detention with a finger wagging and a wink.
I was numb as we walked down the hall
to the science lab. Things were starting to
make sense, but I wasn't at all sure how I felt
about it.

CHAPTER THREE

The only normal thing about Robert Smith is his name. Everything else about the guy is off. In kindergarten he was the kid who ate paste and didn't talk. In first grade he brought in his dead parakeet for show-and-tell. His pants are always too short, he's got major cowlicks, he picks his nose, talks to himself constantly, and on top of all of that, he smells fishy. Over the years he's managed to distinguish himself as the weirdest, craziest, most unappealing character in the whole class. His name never seemed to fit him, so we dubbed him Bob-o early on. Even the teachers call him Bob-o. And this was the guy who shared my birthday.

"He was the only July birthday in the whole bunch other than me," I told Buzz as we took the shortcut through the field and headed for my house.

"Was it the fourteenth?" Buzz asked.

I nodded.

"Now, don't panic or anything. We could still be barking up the wrong tree. Just because he was born on July fourteenth doesn't mean he was born in the same hospital and that you and Bob-o were switched at birth. Maybe he moved here from some other place."

"Or some other planet," I suggested.

"We've got to do a little more digging."

My mother was out shopping, but she'd left a note saying there were cookies in the cookie jar and some kind of punch she'd whipped up in the fridge. The punch was a strange-looking brown mixture with a thick skin on top, so I poured us a couple of glasses of milk. We grabbed some cookies and went up to my room.

"What hospital were you born in, anyway?" Buzz asked.

"Saint Matthew's," I answered.

"Gimme the phone," said Buzz.

I handed him the portable and he punched in three numbers.

"Yes, can I please have the number of Bob-o, I mean *Robert*, Smith?" he said into the receiver.

I grabbed the phone away from him and turned it off.

"He's not listed himself, pea-brain. The number's probably under his father's name."

"Oh, right. What's his father's name?"

"Like I know," I said.

"Like maybe you *should* know considering the gentleman might be your own flesh and blood, weasel-brain."

I pulled the Cedar Springs Middle School directory off the shelf and looked up Bob-o's number. His parents were listed as John and Marie Smith, on North Maple Street. I handed the book to Buzz and watched as he dialed.

"Hello, is this Mrs. Smith?" he said in a phony deep voice. "Wonderful, well this is Mr.—" he looked around the room for inspiration until his eyes settled on my bulletin board—"uh, Mr. Pushpin, I'm calling from Saint Matthew's hospital. . . . uh huh. . . . We're updating our files here at Saint Matt's, and we just need to double-check a couple of things with you, okay? . . . Great, Mrs. Smith. According to our records you gave birth to a son here on July 14, 1986, is that correct? . . . uh huh . . . Robert Louis Smith . . . uh huh, I see." Buzz rolled his eyes at me and gave a thumbs-up sign. "And during the time you were in our hospital was your baby ever out of your sight, say, wrapped up in a little blue blanket in the nursery with a lot of other boy babies that looked *exactly* like him? Huh, what? Pushpin, Mr. Pushpin, whoops, sorry, um, uh—" Buzz grabbed a pencil and began tapping on the receiver with it. "I'm afraid I can't hear you, Mrs. Smith! I'm sorry, but we seem to have a bad connection here! I,

I really have to run now! Thank you *so* much, bye-bye now!" Buzz hung up quickly.

"Mr. Pushpin ?" I said.

"It did the trick, didn't it? You and Bob-o were definitely born in the same place, Guy."

"Did she answer the part about taking her eyes off the baby?" I asked.

"No, that's when she got suspicious and I had to hang up."

We sat there in silence for a minute looking at each other. Could it be true? Was I really Bob-o and Bob-o was actually me?

"I need some air," I said.

"Yeah, let's go to the fort."

We pulled on our jackets and left.

CHAPTER FOUR

Buzz and I built the fort the first summer after we met. We were both eight then, and our carpentry skills were not exactly well honed, but it had held up remarkably well. We'd used scraps of plywood from under his porch, plus a bunch of carpet samples and shingles that had been lying around in my basement. My father had also given us a pile of old records he didn't want anymore, so we nailed those up all over the place too. Over the years it had developed a coating of green moss and a very distinctive odor, but it was a home away from home for both of us. We'd added various comfort features along the way, a couple of beat-up chairs, an orange crate for a table, and a busted TV that we kept in the corner because we both thought it made it feel more homey. Sometimes we slept out in the fort, but mostly we went there for a few hours at a time to talk, or pout, or blow off steam, depending on what was going on with us.

"So, what are you going to do now?" Buzz asked me once we were sitting in the fort with our feet up on the table.

"Man, it reeks in here, doesn't it?" I said, avoiding the question.

"Smells like feet," Buzz said.

"Yours, maybe."

Buzz looked at me.

"Okay, so let me rephrase the question, Guy Wire: What are you going to do after you finish insulting my feet?"

"I don't know," I said, staring at the blank screen on the old TV. "I just don't know."

"Well, I know what I'd do if I was you," Buzz said. "I'd go take a look at Mr. and Mrs. Smith and see if they looked like me."

"Yeah, I guess I could do that."

"Want me to go with you?" Buzz asked.

"Yeah, but not today. I need some time to let it all sink in, you know?"

"Sure. We can go tomorrow if you want. It's Saturday, so they might be out in their yard raking leaves or something."

"Okay. Let's meet on North Maple at ten."

"You want me to bring my binoculars?"

"Whatever."

I didn't sleep well that night. I tossed around for hours and when I finally did drift off, I had a weird dream about trying to comb my hair in the bathroom and not being able to see my reflection in the mirror. I woke up in a sweat and just lay in my bed until it was almost time to go meet Buzz.

"Hey, sleepyhead!" my mother called out to me from her workroom when she heard me pouring a bowl of cereal in the kitchen.

"Hey," I called back.

"Come see what your clever old mom's been up to out here, sweetie. You're going to *love* it."

I carried my bowl of granola out to her room, and what I saw made me furious. There on her workbench was my old baseball-card collection. She'd taken the cards out of the little plastic sleeves and was in the process of gluing them onto a lamp shade.

"Won't this be adorable in your room, Guy?"

She was just starting to squeeze glue onto my Reggie Jackson. I'd spent weeks convincing Buzz to trade that card to me. I snatched it out of my mother's hand and fought back the tears that had sprung up in my eyes.

"Did it ever occur to you, Mom, to ask before you go destroying my private property?" I said through clenched teeth.

She looked genuinely surprised.

"I'm not destroying them, honey, I'm preserving them forever. As art."

"Baseball cards aren't *art*, Mom. They're *baseball* cards. You preserve them by keeping them in albums, which is what I was doing until you went and messed everything up. I want my cards in an album, not on a lamp shade."

"But this way you can see them more—"

"If I want to see them I open up my album and look at them just like a regular person!" I yelled. "But you wouldn't understand that, would you? You don't have any idea what *regular* is, do you? I can't take this anymore. This time you've gone too far!"

"Boy, somebody got up on the wrong side of the bed," my father said from the doorway.

"Wrong side of the *bed*? Try *wrong* side of the *wrong* bed in the *wrong* house in the *wrong family*!" I shouted as I pushed past my father and ran out of the house.

I grabbed my bike out of the garage, skidded down the driveway, and rode off in a fury toward North Maple.

CHAPTER FIVE

Buzz wasn't there yet. I parked my bike on the corner and sat down on the curb to wait. Lawn mowers were buzzing, and I could hear the high pitched squeal of one of those weed choppers going nearby. It was a family block, lots of kids out on tricycles and a basketball hoop in almost every driveway. A real normal street.

The Smiths lived at 2120 North Maple, which I figured was probably the last house on the corner on the left-hand side. I was too far away to tell whether they were out in the yard, but I wanted to wait for Buzz before I moved in for a closer look. Just then he pedaled up to me and jumped off while his bike was still moving. He had his binoculars hanging around his neck.

"Sorry I'm late," he panted.

"You're not. I was early," I said.

"Did you see anything yet?"

"Nope. Their house is down the block on the left. I think it's the white one with the green fence in front."

"So, how do you want to do this?" Buzz asked.

"Well, maybe we should start by riding by and seeing if anybody's outside."

"Good plan."

We pedaled down the block trying to look like we were minding our own business. When we got to the white house with the green fence we were both surprised to see Bob-o out in front on his hands and knees messing with a big pile of wet gray stuff. We kept going until we'd rounded the corner and were out of Bob-o's sight.

"What the heck was he doing?" I asked.

"Maybe he's building a spacecraft to carry

him back to his people."

"I think there's a good chance 'his people' might be hanging out at my house decorating lamp shades," I said. "In which case all he'll need is a bike."

"Did you see Mr. and Mrs. Smith anywhere?" Buzz asked.

"I think I might have heard the mower going in the backyard, but I didn't see anybody."

"Let's go by there again."

"What if Bob-o notices?" I said.

"When has Bob-o ever taken an interest in anything other than getting his knuckles up his nose?" Buzz said with disgust.

"Well, just to be safe why don't we cut over a block and check it out from the back," I suggested.

We bypassed North Maple and rode over to Sycamore. I could see the top of the Smiths' house through a bunch of trees. Buzz and I left our bikes on the sidewalk and pushed our way through some shrubs to the edge of Bob-o's backyard. There was Mr. Smith, pushing the mower, and standing on the steps watering a hanging plant was Bob-o's mother. We crouched down and watched.

"Want the binoculars?" Buzz whispered in my ear.

"We're practically on top of them already. I don't want to look at their earwax, pith-brain, just shut up," I said, my eyes glued to the two people who might actually be my parents.

"Don't be such a turkey," Buzz said, and punched me in the arm.

"Ow!" It didn't hurt that much, but it startled me because I was completely engrossed in scrutinizing the Smiths.

"This is not my idea of a fun way to spend a Saturday morning, you know," Buzz muttered. His feelings were clearly hurt, but I couldn't be bothered with that right now. "I could have gone fishing," he grumbled.

"Shut up, will you," I hissed at him.

"Bite me," Buzz said, and he started to stand up to leave.

At the same moment Buzz stood up, I decided maybe the binoculars might not be such a bad idea, and I reached over to take them. My hand got tangled in the strap and the two of us bumped heads. Buzz lost his balance, and we both tumbled out of the bushes right into the Smiths' backyard.

"Hey, what's going on here?" yelled Mr. Smith as he headed across the yard to where Buzz and I lay sprawled, gasping.

"Think fast," I whispered.

"Uh, hello. We're looking for Bob-o, uh, Robert. Is this his house?"

"It's okay, Marie," Mr. Smith shouted to his wife, who was standing on the steps with her watering can poised in midair. "They're friends of Bobby's."

Buzz and I stood up and brushed ourselves off.

"Yeah, we're friends of Bobby's," Buzz said, nodding a little too enthusiastically.

"I think he's around in the front," said Mr. Smith. "Why don't you go look for him there. I'm sure he'll be delighted to see you two."

Buzz and I headed around the side of the house. As we passed Mrs. Smith she smiled and said, "You're here to see Bobby? Well, isn't that just lovely."

As soon we were out of earshot Buzz said to me, "Yeah, Guy, isn't this just *lovely?*"

CHAPTER SIX

Bob-o was still busy with the pile of wet gray stuff on his front lawn. In fact, he was so engrossed that he didn't notice us even though we were practically on top of him. We stood and watched him for a minute, and then Buzz cleared his throat.

"Ahem." Bob-o didn't look up. "*Ahem*. Hey there, Bob-o, what are you up to, anyway?"

Bob-o looked up. His curly red hair was matted with the gray stuff, and his glasses were so gunked up that he had to squint to make out who was talking to him. He looked at us for a minute with his mouth hanging open and then, without a word, he plunged his hands back into the wet mass and began squeezing it between his fingers. Buzz looked at me and shrugged.

"No point in hanging around here, Guy. He's not talking, and he's disgusting to look at all covered with that glop. I say we am-scray."

"Wait a second, will you?" I said. I looked around. Under a nearby bush I saw a large cardboard box. BUILD YOUR OWN VOLCANO! it said in bright red letters across the front. "So, you're building a volcano, huh, Bob-o?"

Bob-o muttered something unintelligible under his breath and kept mushing his hands around in the glop.

"Well, I like volcanoes as much as the next guy, I guess. Buzz likes 'em too, don't you, Buzzard?"

"Yeah, I like volcanoes. But that looks more like rotten oatmeal than hot lava," said Buzz.

"I don't think that's the lava, Buzz. I think he's trying to build the mountain," I said.

"Looks more like a swamp than a mountain," Buzz offered.

"Too much water," said Bob-o under his breath.

"So, why don't you add more plaster?" I asked.

Bob-o didn't answer me, but he picked up the empty plaster bag and shook it fruitlessly over the soggy mess.

"How about adding dirt?" suggested Buzz.

Bob-o looked at me and tried to wipe his glasses on his sleeve without taking them off. He ended up making them even dirtier than they'd been before.

"Gimme that bucket," said Buzz, taking charge.

He ran over and scooped a pailful of black dirt out of Mrs. Smith's flower bed and brought it over to Bob-o, who dumped it into the mix and began to work it in with his hands.

"Needs more," Buzz said, and handed the bucket to me.

It took four more loads of dirt to attain the perfect consistency to build the mountain. By that time Buzz and I were up to our elbows squishing and squeezing the disgusting but irresistible stuff right along with Bob-o. Despite the fact that Bob-o didn't say a word and there was a pronounced smell of fish coming from his direction, we worked hard together for an hour, ending up with an impressive mottled mound that rose about three feet off the ground. It was not as perfectly formed as the mountain in the picture on the box, but we all agreed that the dirt made it look far more authentic. When we'd packed on the last handful of dirty plaster, Bob-o inserted a long plastic tube into the center of the mound and smoothed over the edges so it didn't show at the top.

"Mount Bob-o!" declared Buzz as we proudly surveyed our handiwork. "When will she blow?"

"It says here that it's supposed to dry for

three days and then you can make it erupt,"
I said, reading the instructions on the back of
the box.

Just then Mrs. Smith came around the
side of the house.

She didn't comment on our volcano at all,
but she gave us a nice big smile before going
to work pulling up a large dandelion with a
gardening claw.

Without a word Bob-o stood up, walked
into the house, and closed the door behind
him. Buzz looked at me and shrugged.

Mrs. Smith finally conquered the stubborn
weed and moved across the yard in search of
her next victim. Suddenly I remembered the
whole reason I was there to begin with. I
watched Mrs. Smith chopping away with her
claw, and I took a quick inventory. Brown hair,
straight as a board. Just like mine. Green eyes.
Like mine. Navy-blue sweat pants and a plain
white T-shirt. My favorite color combination.
Then I noticed she was holding the gardening claw in her left hand. I gasped.

"Are you a lefty, Mrs. Smith?" I called out to her.

"A lefty? Why, yes, as a matter of fact, I am," she said.

"Sheesh, Guy. Just like you," said Buzz softly.

"Yeah, just like me," I said.

We rinsed off our hands with the garden hose. Bob-o never came back out. I wanted to check out Mr. Smith more closely—I thought I might have noticed a dimple in his chin that looked like mine—but he must have gone inside too. Mrs. Smith finished pulling dandelions and headed around to the back again.

"I know who you are now," she said, looking at me with her head tipped to the side. "You're the Strang boy, aren't you?"

"Yeah, I'm Guy," I said.

"Isn't that lovely," she said sort of absent-mindedly as she disappeared around the corner of the house.

"Seems like a very nice lady," said Buzz.

"Uh huh," I said.

"I don't suppose you're in the mood for double fries and a dog," said Buzz.

"I'm not hungry," I said.

"I don't blame you," said Buzz as he patted my shoulder. "I guess you noticed, she looks just like you. And the left-handed thing. Sheesh. "

We hopped on our bikes and rode in silence until we reached my corner.

"Sure you don't want a dog?" asked Buzz. "My treat."

I shook my head, waved, and turned up the street. As I neared my house, I could not believe my eyes.

CHAPTER SEVEN

My parents were in the front yard. Dad was standing on a crate posing in his bathing suit. He had on black socks and his brown loafers. Mom, wearing a black garbage bag with holes cut out for her head and arms, was chipping at a huge block of ice with a hammer and chisel. The grass around the ice block was soggy, so she wore a pair of rubber flippers; and to protect her eyes from the flying ice chips, swim goggles.

My father's face lit up when he saw me.

"Hey, Guy! Look, your mother's immortalizing me in ice," he called.

"Uh huh," I said as I wheeled my bike into the garage and leaned it against the back wall. I let myself in the side door so that I didn't have to see the spectacle known as my family out there on display for all the world to see. I wasn't sure how much more humiliation I could stand.

I seriously considered going upstairs and climbing into my bed with my clothes on, pulling the covers over my head, and staying there until I turned eighteen and could legally move out. I also thought about dialing Bob-o's number and begging Mrs. Smith—"Mom"—to come and straighten out this horrible mix-up. Instead, I poured myself a bowl of granola, pulled the family photo album off the shelf, and went out into the backyard to swing in the hammock and study photographs from the early days, hoping they might shed some light on the situation.

I could hear my mother chipping away at the ice and the murmur of my parents' voices drifting through the air as I opened the album. The first few pages were full of sepia-colored photos of ancient relatives in top hats and long white dresses. I recognized my grandparents, smiling stiffly on their wedding day. It was hard to believe that Grandpa Strang had ever actually had hair. Then there was my mother graduating from high school, looking almost normal in her cap and gown until you noticed she had painted her feet to look as if she was wearing shoes even though she was actually barefoot. There was Dad in a scout uniform standing proudly next to a tepee he'd obviously made out of newspapers and a bunch of coat hangers. He looked almost exactly the same because he was wearing nerdy black-framed glasses identical to the ones he still wears, and his pants, as usual, were about three inches too short. I hurried through my parents' wedding photos because seeing them looking all moony-eyed at each other—my father for some reason wearing a ridiculous gold turban and my mother a wreath of real grapes on her head—made my stomach ache.

There were a couple of pictures of my mother pregnant and then, all of a sudden, there I was. Pink and bald and bawling. There were many pictures of my mother holding me, walking me, bathing me, burping me. It appeared that I was usually either asleep or crying in the first few months of my life. As I got a little older, except for the way they combed my hair into a kind of Dairy Queen curlicue on top of my head, I looked like a pretty regular baby. But once I was up and on my feet the pictures began to tell a different story.

First of all, there were the Halloween costumes—homemade, of course. One photograph showed me covered, head to toe, with gray fuzz. The caption read GUY, AGE 4. "LINT." They had actually dressed me up as a lint ball and sent me out trick-or-treating. There were also many shots of birthday celebrations, at which my father performed magic tricks (including the infamous "snort the oyster") and my mother immortalized me on the top of one birthday cake after another. On one particularly embarrassing occasion, my eighth birthday, she had used tan frosting to create a naked birthday boy complete with a pink gumdrop to represent my "outie" belly-button. Was nothing sacred?

As I gazed at the rock-solid proof of my insane upbringing I heard the flip-flopping of my mother approaching in her swim fins.

"Guy, sweetie," she said, "come see the ice sculpture. It's a trip."

"Not a trip I'm interested in taking," I said without looking up.

My mother pulled the goggles up onto her forehead and looked at me. "Something the matter?"

"Look at yourself, Lorraine," I answered. "You look like something from *Sea Hunt.*"

"Oh, I *loved Sea Hunt.*" She shooed a horsefly away with one of her fins. "Hey, how do you know about that show, and why are you calling me 'Lorraine' all of a sudden?"

"They show *Sea Hunt* all the time on the oldies rerun channel, and in case you've forgotten, your name is Lorraine."

"Oh, I thought I was 'Mom,'" she said.

"So did I," I said quietly.

"Listen, Guy, your dad and I had a great idea. We thought it might be fun to have a party tonight, you know, invite a few people over for a barbecue? And here's the kicker. We're going to fill the wading pool with lemonade and float your father in it. What do you think?"

"Dad's going to float in the pool?"

"Not the real Dad, the ice sculpture Dad. It'll give me a chance to show it off."

"Well, count me out," I said as I swung my legs over the edge of the hammock and hopped out.

My mother put her hands on her hips. "Are you still mad about the lamp shade?" she asked. "Is that what this is all about?"

"That's only part of it, just the tip of the iceberg," I said. "Do you have any idea what it feels like to be dressed up as a lint ball and sent out in public? Or what it's like to see yourself naked on top of a cake being served to your entire second-grade class? No one eats raw hot dogs for lunch, do you realize that?" My mother didn't say anything. "I like peanut butter and jelly, and white underwear. I like Superman, not Lee Trevino. I like blue and white, not purple and orange, and I don't like my prized possessions glued to household appliances."

"But white underwear is so *boring*, honey."

"Then I guess I'm boring," I said. "And you know what? If you want someone more exotic than me for a son, maybe you should have been more careful about which little bundle of joy you brought home from the hospital that hot July afternoon. Did you ever think about that, *Lorraine*?"

"What in the world are you talking . . ."

But I was already halfway across the yard, propelled by my anger and the need to straighten out this ridiculous sham of a life I was leading.

CHAPTER EIGHT

I stayed up in my room for the rest of the afternoon. I heard my parents dragging the wading pool off the rafters in the garage and across the backyard to the patio. I listened as they made preparations for their little "shindig," as my mother kept calling it.

"How many gallons of lemonade do you think it'll take to fill it up, Wuckums?" my mother called to my father. His name is William, but he'd had trouble pronouncing it as a child and had inadvertently nicknamed himself "Wuckums" for life.

"Just dump in all of the containers and fill it with the hose," he called back. "If it's too weak I'll run down to the store and get more."

My father got the grill going, and soon the odor of barbecued chicken wafted up into my room. I put the pillow over my head and ignored my rumbling stomach. I was not going to this party no matter what. Even with my head covered I could hear my mother squealing as she and my father carried the ice sculpture from the front yard to the back.

"Oooh, you're giving me goose bumps, Wuckums!" she cried.

Then I heard a loud splash as they tossed my mother's work of art into the pool.

"You know, dear, it really does look like me. Especially around the ears," my father boomed cheerfully.

Pretty soon I heard people arriving. I recognized the voices. Leo and Emma Biedermeyer, the two wackos who owned the art-supply shop in town. Petra Vidnowich, an accomplished classical pianist who taught all the kids in the neighborhood even though she hated children. Sammy and Val, our next-door neighbors, who liked my parents because they didn't complain when their cat used my old sandbox for a toilet. And then I heard a voice I knew I recognized, but I couldn't quite place.

"Long time no see, William. Long time no see."

"Call me Wuckums, John. Everybody else does."

"Really? Okay . . . Wuckums," said the man tentatively.

John. Who was John? I racked my brain but came up empty.

"Yoo-hoo, Marie, come and take a look at my latest work of art. And while you're at it, how about a glass of lemonade?" called my mother.

Marie? John and Marie? Wait. It couldn't be. I jumped off the bed and raced over to the window just in time to see Bob-o's mother accepting a glass of lemonade from my mother. Or was it the other way around? Good grief, my real mother and my supposed mother, face-to-face in my own backyard.

"I suddenly remembered that incredible barbecue sauce you made years ago and I thought, 'You know, Lorraine, you should just call up that Marie Smith and ask her for the recipe. So what if you haven't talked to her in umpteen years, we had *babies* together for gosh sake, she'll give you the recipe.' And I figured if I was serving your sauce, the least we could do was invite you and John over to sample it."

I couldn't believe my ears.

"Lovely of you, Lorraine," said Mrs. Smith, laughing nervously. "I'm just surprised you remembered the sauce—why it must have been almost twelve years ago that we all got together for that picnic."

"Right after the boys were born," said my mother.

"Time flies," said Mrs. Smith.

Personally, at that particular moment I felt as if time was standing still. They actually *knew* each other and they knew they'd both had boys at the same time. We'd all gone on a picnic together! It was shocking. Just then I heard a noise behind me and I spun around to find Bob-o Smith standing in my doorway with his finger up his nose.

CHAPTER NINE

"This is a no-picking zone, Bob-o," I said.

"Huh?" he said, still digging around in his nose.

"DON'T PICK YOUR NOSE IN MY ROOM!" I shouted.

Bob-o slowly removed his finger from his nostril, and as I watched in horror, he wiped it on the leg of his jeans.

"Didn't your mother ever teach you how to use a tissue, Bob-o?" I asked.

He just stared at me.

"Look, I don't know what the deal is with you, but you're standing here in my room so I might as well take advantage of that fact and drop my big bomb," I said.

Bob-o said nothing.

"Okay, there's something you should know, Bob-o. Something very serious and very weird and very, well, hard to believe."

Bob-o looked at me and started to scratch his nose.

"Put your hands in your pockets!" I barked.

He did.

"Okay, here goes, I'm about to tell you something that is going to change your life forever. Something that you won't believe at first, but I will be able to prove to you."

Bob-o blinked slowly behind his thick glasses. I took a deep breath.

"We have the same birthday, Bob-o—July fourteenth."

Bob-o wrinkled his nose but didn't make a move to scratch it.

"And we were born in the same hospital—Saint Matthew's."

"So?" said Bob-o. "My mother told me that in the car on the way over here. She said that she and your mom shared the same room at the hospital."

I don't know which was more amazing— that Bob-o had spoken to me out loud in full sentences or the shocking thing he had just told me.

"You're kidding!" I gasped.

"I thought you said you had proof about something weird." He turned around and headed for the door.

"Wait. My proof is standing out in the backyard right now. Come over here." I grabbed the back of Bob-o's shirt and pulled him backward toward my window. I spun him around and pointed to the patio, where my mother and father were getting ready to do the limbo while their guests, including John and Marie Smith, looked on politely. "Look at them," I ordered.

Bob-o watched silently as my father attempted to slip his bulging belly under the limbo bar (an old bamboo fishing pole held at one end by my mother).

"Suck it in and wiggle your hips, Wuckums!" my mother shrieked. "Come on, hoochy-koochy man, put a little Elvis in your pelvis!"

Bob-o snickered.

"Shh. Keep watching."

My father managed to go under the bar—mostly because my mother cheated and lifted it higher so his gut could pass under it. Then it was her turn.

"Cha-cha-cha-cha-cha-CHA . . ." My mother began to sing and dance a demented little number that involved sticking her rear end out and pursing her lips. At one point she bumped into Mr. Smith so hard that she knocked him off balance and his arm went into the lemonade-filled wading pool up to his elbow. Mrs. Smith rushed over with some napkins to help dry him off while my mother, oblivious to her wet guest, contin- ued to dance. Finally she made a big show of bending way over backward and sliding under the fishing pole. As soon as she was done my father dropped the pole and applauded wildly. Then my mother ran over and hopped on his back so he could run, carrying her piggyback around the backyard for a minute.

"What do you think of them, Bob-o?" I asked. He shrugged. "Do you think they're weird?" He shrugged again. "Embarrassingly freakish?" I asked.

"Not particularly," he said. "I think they're sort of . . . cool."

"Exactly. And there's your proof," I said as I flopped down on my bed, partly because I'd made my point and partly because Bob-o was smelling fishy and I needed some breathing room.

"Proof of what?" asked Bob-o, coming dangerously within whiffing distance again.

"Proof of the fact that you and I were switched at birth."

Bob-o started to protest, but I stopped him before the words actually made it out of his mouth.

"Look at yourself and look at my folks. Don't you see the similarity?" I asked. "Sure, there's the bad eyesight, the high-water pants and the red hair, but there's something much bigger than that. You're all kind of, well, forgive me for being blunt, Bob-o, but you're all kind of *different* in the same way. You know?"

"And you think they're really my—" Bob-o said.

I nodded. "And your mom and dad are really my mom and dad too—all the signs point to that."

"They do?" said Bob-o.

"Sure. There's the straight brown hair and the left-handedness, but that's not the most important thing—your parents are completely normal, Bob-o," I said. "Normal, predictable, ordinary, regular. Like me, right?"

Bob-o sort of half shrugged, half nodded in response.

"Don't you get it? They shared the same *room* when we were born. Do you have any idea how easy it would be to mix up a couple of babies if you were taking them to the same room?"

Bob-o sat down on the foot of my bed and started to scratch his nose. I gave him a sharp look, and he put his hands back in his pockets. He smelled terrible. I had to finish up this discussion soon or I was going to pass out.

"Do you believe me now?" I asked. Bob-o did his half shrug, half nod again. Just then I heard a loud belch. Buzz stood in the doorway with his hands on his hips and an annoyed look on his face.

"Excuuuuse me," he said, "but since when do you have parties and not invite me?"

"This is no party, Buzzard. This is life and death."

"Oh," said Buzz as he came over and sat on the edge of the bed, "in that case I'm no longer offended, just curious. Sheesh, it smells like Sea World on a hot day in here."

"I just clued Bob-o in about the baby mix-up and I'm glad you're here, because we could use a little expert advice."

"That's my specialty," said Buzz as he snatched up a magazine and started fanning fresh air in through the open window.

"We need to figure out a way to tell our parents," I said.

Buzz put down the magazine and pulled a yo-yo out of his pocket. He fiddled with the string, trying to fit his finger through the loop.

"Okay," he said. "The main thing you have to remember about parents is that they're not happy unless they think they're in the driver's seat, and you can't tell them anything because they think they know everything already." He finally got his finger through the loop and executed a couple of wobbly tosses of the yo-yo. "So, if you go down there right now and say 'Look, there's been this terrible mix-up and you've been raising the wrong kids,' they're just going to laugh and ignore you."

"So, what do you suggest?" I asked.

Buzz tried to rock the cradle, but he

screwed up and the yo-yo got tangled.

"Obviously, what you're going to have to do is trick them into figuring this thing out for themselves," he said as he tried in vain to untangle the string.

Bob-o was sitting on my bed fidgeting and muttering to himself.

"What are you muttering about? If you have something to say about all of this, why don't you say it out loud," Buzz said.

"Why would anyone in their right mind want to be me?" Bob-o asked so loud and clear that both Buzz and I jumped.

Buzz snorted. "He doesn't want to be *you*, Bob-o, he wants to be himself. He just wants to be that self in the right home."

"Your home looks okay to me," said Bob-o, looking around. "Why don't you pick somebody more exciting to be, like a movie star with a swimming pool or one of those big wrestling guys with all the muscles?" He pulled his neck down into his shoulders, grimaced, and went into a classic muscleman pose that looked so ridiculous I had to laugh.

"I'm glad you two are hitting it off so well all of a sudden, but could we get back to the matter at hand, please?" said Buzz, giving me a look. "Your parents have spent years trying to fit a square peg in a round hole, right, Guy? And Bob-o's parents have been dealing with a round peg and a square hole."

I nodded.

"What you need to do is bring the square peg to the square hole and the round peg to the round hole, so they can see what it feels like to be dealing with the right pegs and the right holes."

"How do we do that?" I asked.

"You switch places," said Buzz simply.

"Like I said," said Bob-o. "Wouldn't you rather be—" and he went into his muscle-man pose again, baring his teeth and twisting his wrists to make his puny little biceps jump up and down. It really was funny. I would have laughed, but Buzz looked annoyed, so instead I said, "You're nuts. We don't exactly look alike, you know. Don't you think they'd notice?"

"What do you take me for, Guy, an idiot? Tell them it's a homework assignment for Humanities—you're trying to prove whether it's true what they say about how you have to walk a mile in another man's shoes to really know how he feels. Then, you move into each other's houses, cozy up to your real folks, drop a few hints, and before you know it they put two and two together and—*ta-da!* You guys end up living happily ever after in your rightful homes."

"You know, Buzzy, for an idiot you're pretty brilliant," I said.

"Why, that tongue of yours could charm the skin right off a rattlesnake, do you know that, sonny?" Buzz said, putting on his accent just like he'd done for Mrs. Dipnower.

Bob-o giggled.

"Come on, let's get out of here and get some fresh air," I said.

"Yeah, let's go to the fort," said Buzz.

"Cool!" said Bob-o, jumping to his feet.

Buzz and I exchanged a look. We'd never allowed anyone else in the fort, and Bob-o certainly wasn't high on our list of people we might be interested in bending the rules for. But he seemed so excited that neither of us had the heart to disappoint him, so the three of us headed off, stopping briefly in the back-yard to grab a couple of chicken legs and some lemonade.

CHAPTER TEN

As we walked through the field toward the fort, Buzz sidled up alongside me and whispered in my ear, "I hope he isn't going to pick his nose in the fort."

"As long as he keeps his hands in his pockets, it shouldn't be a problem," I said.

"What about the stink?" he asked.

"The fort smells like an old sock anyway," I said.

"Great. Now it'll smell like an old sock with a dead fish in it. Nice combo."

We walked on in silence for a little while. Bob-o was lagging behind, kicking stones as he went. Every now and then one of the rocks would skitter up the path and clip one of us in the heel, but since it didn't really hurt we didn't bother to tell him to knock it off.

"You know, Guy," said Buzz as we neared the fort. "I didn't think of this before, but if you switch places with Bob-o you're going to have to sleep in his bed."

I hadn't thought of that either.

"We'll just have to make a deal that each of us will clean our rooms and change the sheets before we make the switch," I said. "To tell you the truth, I'm more worried about the bigger issues."

"You mean like how you're going to get his parents, I mean *your* parents, well, anyway, *them*, to figure out the truth about you guys getting switched?"

"Yeah."

When we reached the fort, Bob-o caught up to us and we gave him the grand tour. He must have remembered the hands-in-the-pocket rule from his visit to my room and figured it would hold true for the fort as well, because he stuck his hands deep into his pockets before he came inside.

"So, what do you think, guys?" said Buzz. "Will a weekend be long enough to accomplish your mission?"

"Should be," I said.

Bob-o shrugged.

"Don't tell your parents about the assignment until Friday morning— that way there won't be time for them to make a stink about it, or snoop around finding out what other parents think of it. Make sure you clean up your rooms and change your sheets and junk before Friday, okay?" Buzz looked pointedly at Bob-o. "Got that? You might want to open a window too."

Bob-o blushed, and for a second I felt bad for him.

"Basically, you'll have Friday night and all day Saturday to point out all the things you have in common with your real parents, then on Sunday—a week from tomorrow—you plant the seed about how babies sometimes get switched at birth, blah, blah, blah. Then all we do is wait for the lightbulbs to go off over their heads."

"Maybe we should go over some of the similarities we want to be pointing out to our new parents," I suggested.

"Good idea. Bob-o, for starters, make sure you dress the way you always do, because that's a big thing you and Guy's parents have in common," Buzz said.

"And don't change your hair," I added.

Bob-o checked out his reflection in the screen on the old TV, carefully studying the cowlicks that stuck out in all directions like a pinwheel. Then he puckered up his lips, put his hands on his hips, and did an exaggerated fashion model pose. I laughed out loud, and so did Buzz, in spite of himself.

"The beauty of this whole thing is that it's all genetic, Bob-o," I said. "It's not your fault that you march to a different drummer and have a wacky sense of style—I mean, you saw my mother tonight. You're going to be happy with her, Bob-o, she's very—"

"Colorful," Buzz interjected. "And so is Wuckums. Wait'll you get a load of the oyster trick. You're gonna love the Strangs, Bob-o. Now, Guy, you already know you need to make a big deal of that left-handed thing, and just be as normal as you always are, right?"

"Do you have any pointers for me about how to act around your mom and dad?" I asked Bob-o. He turned away from his reflection very slowly and looked at me for a minute.

"They don't notice *anything*. I once spoke in a Swedish accent for a whole day and they never said a word. They're just going to leave you alone."

"Sounds like heaven," I said.

"Okay, everybody's clear on the plan, right? Step one, clean up your room; step two, tell your parents about the assignment; step three, move in and impress your new parents with all the traits you have in common; step four, plant the seed for the switched-at-birth scenario; step five, wait for the lightbulbs to go on."

Bob-o and I both nodded as Buzz went down the list.

"What are you going to be doing?" I asked Buzz.

"I'm going to be monitoring the situation, making sure everything goes smoothly."

"Do you really think this plan is going to work?" I asked as we left the fort and headed back to my house with Bob-o bringing up the rear again.

"Sure it is. I thought of it, didn't I? And you said yourself that for an idiot I'm pretty brilliant," Buzz pointed out.

"Well, I have no idea how this whole thing is going to turn out," I said, "but I do know this—I've been living a lie for the past eleven years, and it's high time I did something about it."

CHAPTER ELEVEN

Getting my parents to agree to host Bob-o for the weekend was a cinch. My mother was so thrilled that I was letting her in on something having to do with school that she could barely contain herself. I basically stopped letting her help me with homework back in second grade when I discovered that I could do it faster without her "help." Dad said he thought it was a very interesting assignment and wondered if the parents would be invited to come in and share their experiences with the class. I told him I thought that was unlikely, which is what is known as a major understatement.

Bob-o's parents were fine with the

arrangement too. My mother and Mrs. Smith had several phone conversations working out the details of what we would need to bring with us, and before I knew it I was standing on the porch of 2120 North Maple Street waving good-bye as my parents drove off with Bob-o in the backseat hanging his head out of the window like a dog.

Mr. and Mrs. Smith told me to go upstairs and put my stuff away. Bob-o had done a pretty good job of cleaning up his room, and I was relieved to find that there were clean sheets on the bed and only a hint of fishiness in the air. He'd left me a note explaining that it was fine for me to touch his stuff if I wanted to and telling me that if I felt like erupting the volcano, it was down in the basement with the instructions stuck in the top of it. He was a lot more talkative on paper than in person. At the top of the note he'd drawn a little picture of himself doing the muscleman pose. I laughed, kicked off my shoes, and lay down on the bed to daydream for a while about what it would have been like to have grown up in this room instead of my own. Boy, was it peaceful. I could hear the clock ticking and other than that, not a whole lot. It was never this quiet at my house. My mother was constantly singing or banging or clicking around, and once my father came home from work the two of them never stopped laughing and yacking. The Smiths' house, on the other hand, was the kind of place where a person could be alone with his thoughts, and since I had a lot to think about I felt pretty happy to be there.

I figured it was all right to snoop around a little. I was sure Bob-o was doing the same in my room. I opened his top drawer—white underwear. Second drawer—matched socks. Third drawer—T-shirts, all solid colors. When I opened the bottom drawer I noticed that the fish smell suddenly got much stronger, so I poked around in there a little to see if I could figure out the source of the stink. It didn't take long. Bob-o likes those pants that have a million pockets in them, and when I pulled a pair of his jeans out of the drawer and held them up by the legs, you wouldn't believe what fell out of the pockets.

Little balls of dried-up tuna fish. For some reason Bob-o had balled up tuna fish and stuffed it into his pockets. No wonder he smelled putrid—the guy was a walking compost heap. I stuffed the pants back into the drawer, kicked the fish balls under the dresser with the tip of my shoe, and pushed a big stack of books up against it, hoping that would help keep the smell under control.

I looked around some more, but there wasn't anything cool on Bob-o's shelves. He didn't have any baseball cards or model cars. Pretty much all he had was a million science-fiction paperbacks. On the back of his door was a *Star Trek* calendar with hardly anything written on it. From the looks of it, the only regular social event in Bob-o's life was his weekly visit to the allergist. After I'd been in Bob-o's room for about an hour, Mrs. Smith knocked on the door. I was surprised I hadn't heard her coming. It was probably a combination of the wall-to-wall carpet and the fact that she wore quiet shoes. She didn't actually open the door, she just spoke to me through it.

"I thought I should let you know that we eat dinner at six fifteen, dear, so if you're hungry now you might want to go downstairs and have a snack," she said. I told her that I wasn't really hungry yet, and she said she hoped I liked beef stew because that's what they always have on Friday nights. Once we'd squared away the dinner menu, she went down the hall and I heard her close her bedroom door behind her. There was nothing left to do in Bob-o's room, so I decided to go downstairs and check out the volcano.

The basement light was on already, and I could hear Mr. Smith puttering around down there. I went down and asked him if it was okay for me to erupt the volcano, which was sitting in the corner near the washing machine. He was very busy fiddling around with an old toaster oven he'd taken apart, so it took him a minute before he even answered me.

"Tell you what, young man," he said, "that thing makes an awful stink when you set it off. How would it be if you find something else to do instead?"

"Okay," I said. I thought maybe I might hang around a little longer down there and try to impress him with how normal I was, but he was sort of bent over his workbench with his back to me and I got the feeling he didn't want to talk. I went back upstairs and tried to watch a little TV, but I was too restless to sit still for long. I found myself wondering what Bob-o was up to at my house. I wondered if my mother had tie-dyed his underwear yet or if my dad was doing his magic tricks for him.

The phone rang, which made me jump about a mile since it was so quiet around there. Mrs. Smith called down to me, "Guy, telephone call for you. Someone named Buzz."

I took the call in the kitchen.

"Hey, Buzz," I said, glad to hear his voice on the other end.

"Hey, big guy, how's it going?"

"Great. Very peaceful. Very normal."

"Bob-o's room okay?" he asked.

"A little fishy, but otherwise okay," I said.

"Good. Sounds like you've got things under control, so I'm gonna go check on Bob-o. I'm thinking maybe I better ride over there and sneak in the back 'cause if I call, your mom's gonna ask me whose shoes I'm walking in this weekend and that could get complicated. I wouldn't want to blow this thing for you."

"Right."

"Remember, you've got tonight and all day tomorrow to play up the genetic-link thing, okay? Show them how totally normal you are, and do everything with your left hand, okay?"

"Okay," I said.

"'Bye, Guy."

I hung up the phone and stood in the kitchen looking at Mrs. Smith's copper-bottomed pans hanging neatly on the wall next to the stove. There was one empty spot where I could tell the stew pot simmering on the back burner normally hung. There was a cookie jar on the counter, but when I looked inside, it was empty. I walked back out into the living room and ran into Mrs. Smith coming down the stairs. I jumped. I was having a very hard time getting used to the fact that you never heard this woman coming.

"I hope you're making yourself at home, dear," she said, patting my arm as she went past me into the kitchen. I followed her.

"It's a very nice home you have here, Mrs. Smith," I said. "Very normal."

"Cedar Springs is a lovely place to live," she said as she lifted the lid off the stew and stirred it around a little.

I figured this might be a good opportunity to point out a few of those similarities between us, so I sat down on the tall kitchen stool and dove in.

"So, Mrs. Smith, I notice that you have very straight hair. Do you find it gives you problems in the winter time?" I asked.

"Not really, dear," she said as she opened a cupboard and rummaged around in the spice bottles.

"Because, well, I find I get a lot of static when I take off my hat for instance. You know, my hair stands straight up. I thought maybe since your hair is just like mine, maybe you—"

"I never wear hats," she said as she sprinkled something brown into the stew.

"How about being left-handed?" I said. "Does that ever inconvenience you in any way, because I find sometimes I—"

"No—no, it never bothers me," she said as she picked up the spoon and began to stir again. Then she stopped stirring and looked over her shoulder at me. "Say, aren't you and Bobby supposed to be walking around in each other's shoes this weekend—wasn't that the assignment?"

"Uh, yeah," I answered carefully.

"Well, in that case," she said as she tapped the spoon sharply on the edge of the pot, "you might as well run along now, dear, because Bobby would never stand here chatting with me while I cook. I'll call you when dinner's on the table, okey dokey?" Mrs. Smith smiled a tight little smile that made her eyes into little slits, and then she turned her attention back to the stew.

My mother likes to have company in the kitchen when she cooks, but clearly Mrs. Smith was more of a solitary chef. I went back up to Bob-o's room and tried to read a couple of his science-fiction books. Too many aliens and weird slimy creatures for my taste, and besides, now that I knew about the tuna balls under the dresser, I kept smelling fish even though it was probably mostly in my mind. I wondered what Bob-o was doing at my house. I thought about calling him, but figured it would be safer to leave it up to Buzz to check on how things were going on that end.

At six fifteen on the dot Mrs. Smith called me down to dinner. Mr. Smith sat at one end of the table and Mrs. Smith sat at the other. I took a wild guess and figured the place set on the side was for me. The stew was pretty good and so was the salad. My mother has a habit of putting unusual things in salad, like seaweed and cut-up licorice, but the Smiths' salad was your basic lettuce and carrots—no surprises. For a while I was happy just to sit there and eat. Nobody said very much except for "Pass the salt, please," and other stuff like that. I knew I was supposed to be planting seeds all over the place, but I was having a hard time figuring out how to do it other than to keep reaching for things with my left hand.

Now that Mr. Smith was sitting right near

me, I had a good opportunity to check out the dimple in his chin. It was exactly like mine, so I figured that was as good a place as any to start.

"That's a very unusual dimple you have in your chin, Mr. Smith," I said.

"Thank you," he said as he buttered a roll and bit into it.

"You probably didn't notice, but I have one almost exactly like it myself," I said, thrusting my chin in his direction.

"Very nice stew, Marie," said Mr. Smith without looking at my chin.

"Some people think that a chin dimple is the same thing as a cleft chin," I continued, "but as you probably know, they're not the same at all." Mrs. Smith refilled Mr. Smith's bowl and sat back down. This was a lot harder than I had anticipated. I couldn't tell if they were actually listening, but I went on anyway. "You know, things like dimples are a genetic trait that can be passed down from one generation to the next. Like straight brown hair. And left-handedness. It must be very hard for you to look at Bob-o with his curly red hair and his glasses and his unusual, um, unusual-*ness* and not to think, 'Wow, this kid practically doesn't even look *related* to us at all, does he?''

Mr. Smith put down his spoon and looked right at me. Holy cow, I could practically see the lightbulb going on over his head! This was it, and I was ahead of schedule. They weren't supposed to figure it all out until Sunday, but here it was Friday night and the pieces were falling into place perfectly. I guess some things are just too obvious to go unnoticed.

"Mrs. Smith makes the best darned apple crisp in town, young man. Would you like to try some?'' he said.

That was it? Here I thought he was realizing that I was his long-lost son, but all he was doing was thinking about dessert? Surely Mrs. Smith was catching my drift. I turned to her and in desperation blurted out, "Didn't it ever occur to you that when the nurse brought Bob-o and me in to you and my mom when you were sharing that room in the hospital that maybe by mistake she got us—"

The phone rang before I could finish. Mr. Smith answered it in the kitchen and handed the phone to me. It was Buzz, and he was out of breath.

"Guy, it's Buzz," he panted. "You're not going to believe what's going on at your house."

CHAPTER TWELVE

"It's nuts over there, Guy, positively nuts!"

"What's happening?" I asked as I pulled the phone around the corner and into the hall closet so that Mr. and Mrs. Smith couldn't overhear the conversation.

"Well, for starters, your mother's reinventing Bob-o."

"What are you talking about?"

"She's giving him a makeover. He looks completely different. His hair is all slicked back just like your dad's, she's dressed him up in a bunch of *your* clothes, and while I was watching she was working on hypnotizing him with a tape recorder and a soup spoon," Buzz said.

"Get out!"

"Get in!" he shouted. "Pretty weird, huh?"

"My mother doesn't know how to hypnotize anybody," I said.

"Tell *her* that."

"What about my dad, what was he doing?"

"Well, I couldn't really tell because I was spying on them through the window and the stupid curtains kept blowing in my face, but I think he was in charge of the new hairdo."

"Was Bob-o really wearing my clothes?" I asked.

"Yep. You know, when his pants are long enough to cover his socks he looks a lot more normal," Buzz said.

A terrible thought suddenly occurred to me. "Was he putting anything in his pockets?" I asked. "Oh, man, if he puts tuna fish balls in my pockets I'm gonna kill him."

"Huh?" said Buzz. "He wasn't eating any tuna fish when I was there, just lying on the couch watching your mom wave the soup spoon back and forth in front of his face. But your mom did say something about a cake in the oven and some little celebration she's planning."

"She's probably going to immortalize her new son in frosting," I said.

"Well, just be glad she's not doing it to you. I think your days on top of the cake are numbered, judging by what I saw tonight," said Buzz.

"What do you mean?"

"They looked like one big happy family to me. A matched set. Bob-o all slicked back like a Wuckums-clone and your mom all excited about being reunited with her long-lost little geeky boy."

"Do you really think they know the truth?" I asked.

"Well, if they don't already, it's only a matter of time until they do. Boy, this is going just the way you wanted it to, isn't it?" Buzz said excitedly. "Bob-o's fitting right in at the loony bin, and you're the newest number-one-son over there on normal street, right?"

"Right," I said, but deep inside me something was beginning to feel terribly wrong.

CHAPTER THIRTEEN

Saturday was one of the longest days of my life. The Smiths' house was as quiet as a tomb all morning. Mr. and Mrs. Smith sat on the couch next to each other reading magazines for hours. Mrs. Smith licked her fingertip each time before she turned the page, and Mr. Smith cleared his throat about a million times. I had begun to think that they weren't really all that normal. As far as I'm concerned normal people talk to each other, laugh once in a while, and do stuff other than read and sit around clearing their throats.

After breakfast I dragged the volcano out of the basement, took it out in the backyard, and followed the directions for how to erupt it. What you do is pour baking soda, vinegar, and a little red food coloring down the tube in the middle of the mountain, and it bubbles out of the hole and down the sides. I did it a few times, but it wasn't all that exciting and the smell gave me a splitting headache, so I knocked it off and sat on the steps watching ants. I kept wishing Buzz would call and fill me in on what was happening at my house.

Finally, while we were eating lunch, Buzz called and told me to see if I could borrow Bob-o's bike and meet him over at my house. He said it was urgent. I wolfed down the rest of my sandwich and asked if it was okay to go for a ride on Bob-o's bike. Neither one of them seemed to care, so I went out to the garage, pulled Bob-o's bike out from behind the lawnmower, and rode as fast as I could toward home.

Buzz was waiting for me on my corner. He looked very serious.

"We'd better leave our bikes here and go

the rest of the way on foot," he said.

"What's the matter?" I asked.

"Well, I was over at your house earlier today and I saw something I think you better see."

"What is it?" I asked.

"Follow me, " Buzz said, and his tone of voice made me nervous.

We hid our bikes behind some shrubs and walked through a couple of the neighbors' backyards to get to mine. Then we snuck around the side of the house so we could peek in the living-room window. The lilac bush in front of the window was thick and loaded with big purple flowers. We pushed our way into it, hoping no one would hear the racket as the branches thwapped against the side of the house.

Bob-o was lying on his back on the couch. His face was completely green, his hands were tied in plastic bags, and he wasn't moving.

"He looks dead," I said.

"No kidding," whispered Buzz. "He hasn't

moved since the last time I was here, and that was *hours* ago."

Just then my parents walked into the room. My mother bent over Bob-o and sniffled.

"Poor baby," she said softly.

"Dead to the world," my father said as he put his arm around my mother's shoulders.

"I had to do it," she said. "It wasn't easy, but it had to be done."

"Absolutely," said my father as he led her out of the room.

"What the heck is going on in there?" I asked Buzz.

"Looks to me like they couldn't handle the news, went crazy, and offed their only true son. Looks like you got out of there just in the nick of time, Guy," Buzz said, letting go of the big branch he'd been holding back in order to see in the window. It knocked against the side of the house, letting loose a shower of purple flower petals.

"You're nuts," I said.

"Well, how do you explain it?" he asked.

"I don't know," I said, and I noticed that the feeling I'd had before about things going wrong had shot up a notch in my stomach.

As we crouched by the window looking in at poor Bob-o, I tried to make sense of what was happening to my life. The week before, I had felt completely miserable because I was trapped in the middle of my crazy family. Now I was feeling completely miserable because I felt like an outsider look-ing in at them. It didn't help at all that in the short time I'd been away they appeared to have committed a murder, which meant that they were probably going to be carted off to prison and I would be left to live out the rest of my days with the boring old Smiths.

"This can't be happening," I said as I felt my throat closing up and tears beginning to sting my eyes.

Buzz looked at me and shook his head.

I turned away from the window and was just about to wipe my eyes on my sleeve when I got the shock of my life. Standing right behind us was my mother. She was holding a huge knife, and she didn't look happy at all.

Buzz turned away from the window, and when he got a load of my mom with that knife pointed at me, he went wild. First of all, he started screaming this really high-pitched scream that didn't even sound human, and then he threw himself on my mother and knocked her to the ground. The knife went flying out of her hand, skittered between my legs, and disappeared under the bushes.

"Run, Buzz!" I yelled. Buzz and I took off, running like a couple of maniacs down the street to where we had stashed our bikes. We jumped on and rode for our lives without looking back.

CHAPTER FOURTEEN

"**D**id you see the size of that knife?" Buzz yelled from behind me. "She's gone psycho!"

We were quite a ways from my house before we finally slowed down. Buzz rode up alongside me so we could talk. He was white as a ghost.

"Do you think we ought to call the police?" Buzz asked.

I tried to answer him, but I was too choked up. I started to bawl.

"What am I gonna do?" I wailed. "What am I going to do?"

"Don't worry, Guy," Buzz said, trying to comfort me. "We'll tell somebody and they'll go over there and take care of it. We can call the police from somebody's house or maybe we should go back to Bob-o's house so his folks can help us. Come on." Buzz turned his bike around and headed off toward North Maple Street.

"I wish I'd never figured this thing out," I said as I rode along behind Buzz. "Everything could have just stayed the same. Why did I have to be such an idiot and go messing up the family? So what if they were weird? So what if they snorted oysters and decorated lamp shades? We were a family, weren't we? A perfectly good family, and now everything, everything is ruined."

I cried so hard that by the time we reached Bob-o's house, the whole front of my T-shirt was wet, and a big string of snot was hanging from my nose. Buzz leaned his bike against the garage door and wiped my nose with his shirttail. He was a good friend. Together we walked up the front steps and into the Smiths' quiet little house.

"So where are they?" Buzz asked.

"They're probably reading magazines somewhere," I said.

"Well, they're gonna have plenty of time to read about this in tomorrow's headlines, so we better find them now and get this thing taken care of."

"Mrs. Smith!" I called.

"Call louder," said Buzz.

"Mr. and Mrs. Smith!" I called a little louder this time.

"Lemme do it. HEY, SMITHS!" Buzz shouted at the top of his lungs.

"What in the world is all the racket about?" Mrs. Smith looked all bent out of shape as she came down the stairs with a gardening magazine in her hand. Mr. Smith came in from the living room with his finger stuck in a copy of *Reader's Digest*. They both looked at us like we were crazy.

"Listen," said Buzz. "I don't know where to start, but I think we better call the police because—"

The phone rang and Mr. Smith went to answer it.

"Hello? . . . Yes, yes they're both here. . . . Uh huh . . . yes I will . . . they'll be here . . . all right, William, we'll be waiting."

"William? Was that my dad?" I asked nervously.

"Yes, it was and he did not sound happy at all. He and your mother are coming over here right now—"

"You can't let them do that!" cried Buzz. "She's got a knife!"

"What are you talking about?" said Mrs. Smith. "*Who* has a knife?"

"My mother has a big knife," I said. "Or anyway, she *had* a big knife until Buzz knocked it out of her hands and saved my life, but Bob-o, well, Bob-o wasn't so lucky, he, he—" I started to bawl again.

"I don't know what is going on here, and I'm not sure I want to, so I'm going back in the living room to read in peace until the Strangs arrive. In the meantime, I would very much appreciate it if you two boys would go outside and occupy yourselves with something *quiet*. I, for one, am not in the mood for drama."

"Drama?" said Buzz incredulously as Mr. Smith retreated to the living room. "Try murder."

"Oh, for heaven's sake," said Mrs. Smith. "I'm going to make coffee."

Buzz just stood there with his eyes bugging out.

"I told you they were strange," I said.

"That's putting it mildly. Her wacko so-called son has just been murdered, and she's making coffee," said Buzz.

I heard tires screech as a car rounded the corner at high speed. I knew it was them—and I was right.

My mother came rushing in the front door without even knocking. Her hair was positively wild, and she had dirt all over her face from having been knocked on the ground by Buzz. My dad was right behind her looking more serious than I'd ever seen him look before.

"I am beside myself," said my mother. "Absolutely beside myself. What on *earth* is going on with you, Guy? Some Humanities project this has turned out to be. You're acting like a lunatic, and you"—she pointed a finger at Buzz. "Boy, do you have some explaining to do, mister."

"Me? What about *you*? I saw what you did to Bob-o. I saw it with my own eyes and so did Guy. You offed your long-lost geeky little weirdo son because you couldn't stand the shock, but you're not going to get away with it, Mrs. Strang. Not by a long shot!"

Buzz was riled. My parents just stood there with their mouths hanging open. Mr. and Mrs. Smith, holding their respective magazines, were standing side by side watching the show. Just when I thought it couldn't get any more bizarre, who should walk in but . . . Bob-o. Alive and kicking. Well, to be more accurate, *picking*. There he stood in the doorway with his finger up his nose and a bored look on his face that said "Yeah, yeah this is just like any other day at the Smiths' house."

"Bob-o!" I shouted. "You're alive!"

Bob-o quickly pulled his finger out of his nose and smiled at me. I was so relieved to see him on his feet that I ran over and hugged him in spite of where his finger had been.

"Look at that, Wuckums," my mother said, pointing at Bob-o. "It didn't work."

Buzz, who'd been completely silent since Bob-o had appeared, did something I thought only damsels in distress in fairy tales did. His eyelids fluttered for a second; then his eyes rolled up into his head . . . and he fainted.

CHAPTER FIFTEEN

My dad and Mr. Smith carried Buzz over to the couch, and we put a cold washcloth on his forehead. He wasn't out for very long, but it was still scary seeing my best friend all limp like that. Mrs. Smith brought out the coffee and a plate of crackers, and we all sat down to sort out the truth about what had been going on.

"There was no Humanities project, was there, Guy?" my father said.

I shook my head.

"I don't know where to start," I began, but before too long I'd managed to tell the whole story about how I'd figured out about Bob-o and me being switched at birth. Buzz sat up long enough to put in his two cents about the fact that babies all look alike when they're first born. My mother listened very carefully, and for once she didn't even interrupt, which was pretty surprising. Mr. and Mrs. Smith just sat there having not much of a reaction, which was not very surprising at all. At one point I saw Mr. Smith crack open his magazine and try to read a little when he thought nobody was looking. Bob-o sat on the arm of the couch near Buzz's feet combing his hair with his fingers until whatever semblance of a hairdo my father had created for him was a thing of the past.

When I was all through telling my story my mother looked at me with this really weird crooked smile on her face and said, "Do you honestly think that I'm not your mother, Guy?"

"Well, yeah, I guess I think it's possible," I said. "I mean these things do happen sometimes."

"Marie," my mother said, turning to Mrs.

Smith, who was busying herself putting coasters under everyone's coffee cups and arranging more crackers in a pinwheel on the plate even though no one had eaten any of the ones she'd put out there to begin with. "Do you have a family photo album?"

"Mmm hmm," she said, and moved to the bookcase, where she pulled a large leather-bound photo album from the shelf.

"I'd like to show Guy a picture of Bobby when he was a baby," my mother said quietly.

Mrs. Smith leafed through the book until she found what she was looking for. She handed the book to my mother.

"Come with me, Guy." My mother took the book and carried it out onto the front porch.

At first I hesitated. After all, the woman had been pointing a knife at me only an hour before. Then I figured it was probably safe to follow her, since she obviously hadn't killed Bob-o and she didn't have the knife anymore. I went out onto the porch and sat down beside her on the top step.

"Before I show you this picture, there's something I need to say to you, Guy," she said.

Oh, God, I thought. *Here it comes. She's gonna tell me she's known all along that I'm not really her son.* I felt like I was going to throw up.

"I'm really sorry about the baseball cards."

"Huh?" I said.

"I should never have taken them out of your album without asking you. I'm sorry. Sometimes I just get carried away. Your dad is looking into finding replacements for the ones that are already glued down. The Reggie Johnson—"

"Jackson," I said.

"The Reggie *Jackson* is fine, and I put him back in the album. Can you forgive me?"

"They're just some stupid baseball cards, Mom."

My mother's eyes got all shiny. She put

her arm around my shoulder and pulled me in tight next to her. Then she pointed to a photograph in the book that lay open on her lap. "This is Bobby Smith right after he was born," she said quietly.

"Man, what a weird-looking baby. Why's he all blotchy like that?" I asked.

"Allergies. The poor little thing was splotchy and red from the minute he drew his first breath," my mother said.

"What's with the hair?" I asked.

"Some babies are born with a full head of dark hair like that—usually it falls out later."

"Did I have hair like that?" I asked.

"You were bald as a cue ball. You've seen pictures of yourself, Guy," she said gently.

"Oh, yeah," I said.

"You were sweet and round and pink and bald and the most beautiful baby I'd ever laid eyes on," my mother said, and she had a tiny little catch in her voice like maybe she was going to cry.

"Did you see me right away? Because

maybe Bob-o and I got mixed up when they took us away to clean us up or something," I said.

"I held you in my arms and your dad cut the cord, Guy."

"Gross," I said.

"I nursed you for the first time right there on the delivery table—"

"Yech, Mom, too much information," I protested.

"Guy, I didn't let you out of my sight the entire time I was in the hospital. Poor little Bobby Smith was coming and going all the time for treatments and ointments and what not, while you just lay in my arms staring up at me like a little angel. I felt sorry for Marie. I still do."

"What do you mean?" I asked.

"Guy, Bobby is, well, let's just say he hasn't had an easy time of it. He's always been kind of an odd duck. Marie and John are perfectly nice people, but they don't have a clue when it comes to helping that boy."

"What do you think they should be doing?"

"Paying attention to him. Listening to him. Right from the get-go they refused to really look at him. Now their kid is walking around talking to himself and stuffing his pockets full of rolled-up tuna fish, and they're sitting around with their noses stuck in—"

"—magazines." I finished the sentence for her. "Why does he have tuna fish in his pockets, anyway?" I asked.

"I asked him that. He told me he hates tuna fish, but every day his mother packs him a tuna fish sandwich for lunch. He wads up the tuna and eats the bread."

"Why doesn't he just throw it out?" I asked. "That's what I do with the raw hot dogs."

"You do? Why didn't you tell me not to pack them?"

"I did," I said quietly.

We sat for a minute on the step not saying anything. Finally I got up the nerve to ask,

"How come you said 'it didn't work' when Bob-o walked in, before?"

"He was picking his nose," she said.

"So?" I said.

"I tried to hypnotize him out of that habit," my mother said. "But it didn't work."

"Oh, *that's* what you meant?"

"Uh huh. What did you think I meant?"

"I thought you had tried to kill him, Mom."

"What?!"

"He was green, and Dad said he was dead to the world. I heard him."

"That's just an expression. I tried to hypnotize him to stop him from picking his nose, Guy. Obviously I haven't mastered the technique yet, but I'm starting to get the hang of it. I'll show you when we get home."

Home. I let the word wash over me like a warm wave, but only for a minute. I still had more questions.

"Why did you put Bob-o's hands in plastic bags?" I asked.

"I put an herbal salve on his hands to help

break the picking cycle, and the bags were supposed to keep it from getting all over everything. He fell asleep on the couch and the bags broke open. I was in the kitchen frosting a cake, and by the time I checked on him he'd somehow managed to get himself covered pretty much head to toe with the stuff. My couch will never be the same."

"What were you doing with that knife, Mom?"

"I was cutting the cake when I heard something outside the window. I thought it might be Sammy and Val's cat making a mess in the bushes. Apparently it's tired of your old sandbox and has taken a shine to my lilac bushes, the little poot."

"Were you going to stab it?"

"Of course not. I forgot I even had the knife in my hand. I just ran outside when I heard the commotion in the bushes."

"I thought you were going to kill me," I said, and I was surprised by the flood of emotion I felt as I said it.

My mother put the book down next to her and put her arms around me.

"Apparently a vivid imagination is one of the many genetic traits you failed to notice you had inherited from your parents, you nut," she said.

"Oh, yeah? Name another."

"Ever noticed your father's earlobes?"

"No," I said.

"Well, come take a look. They're notched, and so are yours."

I held the screen door open for my mom, and we went inside to examine those wonderful lobes.

CHAPTER SIXTEEN

The next morning I woke up feeling lighter than I'd felt in a long time. I knew I was where I belonged. I lay in bed, running my fingers over the notches at the tops of my earlobes and listening to the sounds in my house. I could hear my parents laughing in the kitchen. My mother's heels clicked across the floor as she went to turn on the radio. She tuned it in to something jazzy, and I knew when I went down there that she and my dad would probably be dancing.

I got up and opened my top drawer. It was full of brand-new white underwear. I opened the sock drawer—the pairs were still unmatched, but somehow it didn't bother me. I pulled on my clothes and went down to the kitchen. Just as I'd predicted, my mom and dad were doing a tango. Mom's head was thrown back and her eyes were closed. Instead of a red rose between her teeth, she gripped a plastic spatula. Everything was back to normal.

"Good morning!" I called as I grabbed a pancake off the plate, folded it, and shoved it into my mouth.

My parents stopped dancing and watched as I downed another pancake and then gulped some orange juice.

"You feeling all right, son?" my father asked.

"Yeah, Dad, I feel fine."

"We were worried about you yesterday, Guy," he said.

"I know, I was worried about me too. But I'm fine now. Really."

My father reached into his pocket and

handed me a stack of baseball cards.

"I'm still looking for a couple of them."

"Forget about it, Dad. This is fine. Really. Thanks."

I slipped the cards into my back pocket and left my parents standing in the kitchen hand in hand as I headed off to the fort to meet Buzz.

"So, what did I look like when I fainted?" Buzz asked.

"Like sleeping beauty, only ugly." I laughed.

"I'm rubber, you're glue—" he started, but he stopped mid-sentence when Bob-o stuck his head in the door. Buzz and I looked at each other.

"Uh, come on in, Bob-o," I said.

Bob-o stepped inside. He looked different. It took me a minute to figure out that he was wearing new pants—long enough to cover his socks. His hair was also slicked back. He still looked weird, but somehow it was a little better.

"What's up, Bob-o?" Buzz asked.

Bob-o did his shrug thing and stuck his hands in his pockets. Then he looked at me. He said something, but I couldn't hear him.

"Speak up, will ya?" I said.

"I, uh, wanted to thank you," he said.

"Me? For what?" I asked.

"Well, for, for a bunch of stuff."

"Like?"

"Like caring about my being dead even though I wasn't. And letting me come to the fort. And making me realize that they're driving me nuts."

"Who's driving you nuts?" Buzz asked.

"My parents, who do you think?" Bob-o answered.

"You know, Bob-o, I have to agree with you on that one," said Buzz. "Those two are definitely bizarre-o."

"You're telling me. They're turning me into a nervous wreck," said Bob-o. "I had no idea what it felt like to relax until I spent the weekend with your folks, Guy."

I had to laugh. "You found my parents *relaxing*?"

"Yeah. Plus you can hear your mom coming a mile away, which is a very good quality in a mother."

"I know exactly what you're talking about, Bob-o," I said.

"That makes two of you," said Buzz.

I smiled at my old friend.

"One thing, though," Bob-o said seriously. "That oyster trick is really disgusting."

"You get used to it," I said. "Listen, Buzz, would you excuse us for a minute? I want to talk to Bob-o alone."

Buzz didn't looked thrilled, but he went outside and pulled the door closed behind him.

"I owe you an apology," I said. "I'm sorry I dragged you into this mess. I don't know what I was thinking."

"Forget it," he said.

"Can I talk to you about something else?" I asked.

Bob-o gave the half shrug.

"It's about the tuna fish balls."

Bob-o blushed and looked away.

"I think you should tell your mom you want hot lunch from now on. I told mine last night when we got home and she said okay. You and I can brave the mystery meat together."

Bob-o grinned.

"Who knows, maybe it'll put hair on our chests," he said as he stuck out his scrawny chest and flexed his nonexistent muscles.

I laughed and so did he.

"Okay, girls, enough with the private chitchat. Ready or not, here I come!" Buzz called out.

We spent the rest of that afternoon hanging out at the fort, the three of us, talking and laughing and just being regular guys. Well, Bob-o wasn't exactly regular yet, but Buzz and I agreed that his weirdness had a certain charm. When I headed for home at the end of the day, I felt older somehow and a little wiser; and when I pushed open the screen door and saw the cake cooling on the counter, I shouted at the top of my lungs—

"I'm home!"